This book belongs to:

------- ---------

------- ---------

Enid Blyton's
The NEW Adventures of the
Wishing~Chair

Giantland

Illustrated by Erica-Jane Waters

EGMONT

Special thanks to Narinder Dhami

EGMONT

We bring stories to life

The New Adventures of the Wishing-Chair: Giantland
First published in Great Britain 2009
by Egmont UK Limited
239 Kensington High Street
London W8 6SA

Text and illustrations ENID BLYTON® copyright © 2009
Chorion Rights Limited.
All rights reserved.
Illustrations by Erica-Jane Waters

The moral rights of the author and illustrator have been asserted

ISBN 978 1 4052 4390 2

1 3 5 7 9 10 8 6 4 2

www.egmont.co.uk

A CIP catalogue record for this title is available
from the British Library

Printed and bound in Great Britain by Clays Ltd, St Ives plc

Contents

The Characters

Jack

Jessica

Olga

Wishler

Chapter One

'This is *amazing*!' Jessica gasped, her eyes wide as she stared down at the ground below her. 'Look at all these little people from Lilliput – none of them are bigger than my thumb! I'm a real GIANT!'

'Jessica, that sounds really good,' called her brother Jack, who was sprawled on the garden bench.

Wishler the pixie nodded. 'You're going to do very well at the audition for *Gulliver's Travels*.' He was sitting

next to a garden gnome so that if Jack and Jessica's parents glanced out of the window, they'd mistake him for an ornament. Wishler was Jack and Jessica's special secret. The pixie lived in the shed at the bottom of their garden, along with the magical wishing-chair that whisked the three of them off on all sorts of

wonderful adventures.

'I've only got a few more days to learn my lines,' Jessica told them, flipping through the pages of her script. 'I *really* hope I get the part of Gulliver.'

'Go on, do another bit of the play,' Jack said eagerly.

Jessica grinned. 'All right.' She

began tiptoeing carefully around the white daisies that dotted the lawn, pretending they were little people.

Winking at Wishler, Jack stood up and gave Jessica a tiny push. Jessica stumbled, accidentally trampling a daisy.

'Oh no!' Jack was helpless with laughter. 'You've crushed one of the

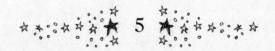

little people!' And he turned and ran

off down the garden.

Laughing too, Jessica chased after him, with Wishler close behind.

Jack dived into the shed, followed by his sister and their pixie friend. He gasped. The colourful paintings that covered the wooden wishing-chair were swirling and changing. 'The wishing-chair must want to take us somewhere!' Jack exclaimed.

'I wonder where it will be?'

Wishler frowned, staring at the paintings. 'It looks like Giantland,' he said slowly with a frown.

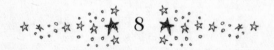

'Giantland!' Jessica gasped. 'So when we go there, *we'll* be the little ones, like the people in Lilliput?'

'We all must be very careful,' Wishler said. 'Giants aren't too fond of little people.'

Jack nodded and sat down on the wishing-chair.

'Don't worry, Wishler, if we're small

we'll be able to hide easily,' Jessica pointed out, joining her brother.

Still looking slightly nervous, the pixie sat down too. They rocked the chair backwards and forwards, and immediately blue sparks began to fizz and crackle around the rockers.

'We wish to go to Giantland!' Jessica shouted excitedly.

Chapter
Two

Jack, Jessica and Wishler closed
their eyes as a flash of blinding blue
light surrounded them. They felt the
wishing-chair soar upwards and spin
around. A second later, the chair
landed with a soft thud, and they

all opened their eyes.

'Look!' Jessica said with her eyes wide. 'We're sitting on a golden cliff!'

Jack peered cautiously over the edge of the shining ledge. 'It's not a cliff, Jessica. The wishing-chair has turned into a big golden throne. We must be in a palace!'

Wishler shook his head as he looked

around. 'We're in a shop's window

display. The clever wishing-chair

has disguised itself to fit in with all the giant furniture that is for sale.'

'It even has a price tag tied to its leg,' Jessica added, pointing.

Jack turned to stare out of the window and felt his mouth drop open. Outside he could see giants *everywhere*. Families were walking along a cobbled street that was lined

with shops and Jack noticed that even the children were as tall as lamp-posts! 'This is *amazing*!' he said, staring at a little girl giant carrying a doll who was bigger than him.

Suddenly, the ground started to shake. Jessica turned round and saw two giant men walking through the

store towards the display window.

'Someone's coming!' she whispered.

'Someone big!'

'That must be the sales-giant and a customer,' Wishler replied. 'Hide!'

Jack, Jessica and Wishler ducked behind the velvet folds of the throne's cushion and peeped round the edges. They saw the sales-giant stare at the

wishing-chair in surprise. He checked the price tag and then, shrugging slightly, pointed at the throne.

'This might be just what you're looking for,' he said to the customer. Behind the cushion, Jack and Jessica clapped their hands over their ears as the giant's voice boomed out.

'Yes, this throne is just the thing!'

the customer said with satisfaction. 'It will be the perfect prize for the winner of the talent competition I'm organising. I'll take it.'

'Very well, sir,' the sales-giant replied.

Clinging on to the folds of the cushion, Jack, Jessica and Wishler glanced at each other in dismay as

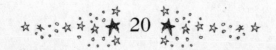

the sales-giant lifted the disguised wishing-chair on to a trolley. The customer then paid for his purchase and wheeled the trolley out of the shop.

'Well, you said you wanted to see Giantland,' Wishler whispered. 'I'm afraid it looks like we don't have any choice!'

Chapter
Three

Turning left out of the shop, the

customer wheeled the throne past

a grocer and Jessica gasped in

amazement as she saw oranges and

apples the size of beach balls. The

throne was then directed along a

bumpy country path bustling with giants.

'Hold on tight!' Jack murmured to Jessica and Wishler. But he'd hardly

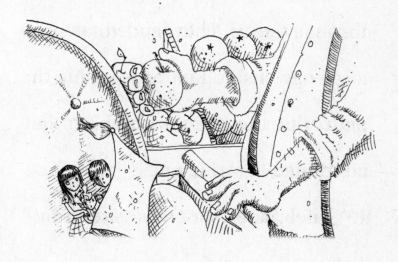

finished speaking when the trolley hit a particularly big bump. Jack, Jessica and Wishler yelped with surprise as they flew off the throne and sailed through the air. They landed safely on a springy cushion of moss beside the path. But the giant with the trolley continued to stride on.

'Quick,' Jack shouted. 'After him!'

'Be careful!' Wishler gasped, as they chased after the wishing-chair. 'There are giants *everywhere*.'

Jack could feel his heart thumping like a drum. All he could see were huge legs tramping along the path. The ground shook beneath his feet and he heard the sound of booming voices all around them.

'It's not safe being a little person in Giantland,' Jessica yelled, jumping out of the way of an enormous boot.

She was beginning to realise exactly how a tiny ant in their back garden must feel.

'He's getting away,' Jack said, as the giant and the wishing-chair disappeared into some woods in the far distance.

'Run faster!' Jessica said.

But by the time they reached the

 27

woods, there was no sign of the giant at all.

'What now?' Jack panted. 'We can't get home without our wishing-chair!'

Suddenly a loud and terrible noise echoed through the woods. Jessica put her hands over her ears.

'What's that?' she shouted. 'It sounds like a foghorn!'

Wishler shook his head, his face looking puzzled.

Jack frowned and then suddenly noticed that his feet felt damp. He glanced down and saw that a stream had appeared from nowhere on the forest floor and they were standing right in the middle of it!

Jessica peered in the direction of

the noise. Through the trees she could

see a young giantess with long black

hair sitting on a grassy hillock. The

giantess was sobbing

loudly, and her

enormous tears were plopping on to the ground, steadily making a stream that flowed towards them.

'I guess that's where the water's coming from,' Jack said, following his sister's gaze.

The giantess then blew her nose loudly into a white handkerchief.

'And *that's* what the awful noise

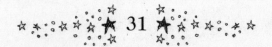

was!' Jessica exclaimed. 'I wonder why she's crying? Maybe we can help.'

'Let's go and talk to her,' Jack suggested to the others.

'Giants don't like little people,' Wishler gasped, rushing after Jack and Jessica as they ran towards the hillock.

Just then the giantess looked

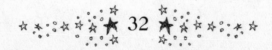

down and spotted the three friends.

'EEEK!' she screamed, almost

bursting Jack and Jessica's

eardrums. 'Mice!

Three mice!'

'We're little

people, not mice,'

Wishler explained

to her, outraged.

'Are you OK?' Jessica asked. 'We wondered why you were crying.'

The giantess frowned suspiciously.

'My mummy told me that little people are horrid,' she snapped. 'And that if I ever saw one I had to stomp on them!'

The giantess slowly raised her enormous foot.

Chapter Four

'Oh, please don't!' Jessica yelled as loud as she could. Beside her, she felt Wishler and Jack trembling. 'Would we have stopped to ask why you were crying if we were horrid?'

To the friends' relief, the giantess

lowered her foot back to the ground.

'That's true,' she said thoughtfully. Then she smiled at them. 'Maybe you're not horrid. My name's Olga.'

'I'm Jack and this is Jessica and Wishler,' Jack said. 'Why are you crying, Olga?'

'I wanted to enter the talent competition at the fairground this evening,' she explained. 'But I'm no good at anything!'

'You mean, you want to win the golden throne?' Jessica asked.

Olga shrugged. 'I don't care about the prize,' she replied. 'I just want to find out what I'm *really* good at.'

'This could be the perfect way to get the wishing-chair back!' Jack

whispered to Wishler and Jessica.

His sister nodded. 'Olga, that throne is actually *our* wishing-chair in disguise,' Jessica said.

'It was the wishing-chair that flew us to Giantland – we can't get home without it,' Wishler explained. 'If we help you with an act for the talent competition, will you give us

the throne if you win?'

Olga looked thoughtful. 'I'd hate to be stranded far away from home,' she said. 'All right, you can have the prize if I do win. But I warn you, I'm no good at *anything*!' She blew her nose again and Wishler was sent flying across the clearing.

He landed safely on a soft daisy.

'I'm sorry, Wishler!' The giantess carefully lifted Wishler up and put him on the ground again.

'Let's decide what you're going to perform at the talent competition,' Jessica said. 'I go to dance class, so I could teach you some steps. Just do what I do.'

'Sure,' Olga agreed eagerly.

Jessica floated across the forest floor, her arms held gracefully above her head. Olga clumped after her.

The giantess made the ground shake so much that Wishler and Jack had to cling on to a tree root.

Jessica did a twirl and Olga tried to do the same, but she spun round too quickly and got her feet in a tangle.

'Sorry, Jessica,' Olga said sadly. 'I'm not very good at this. Did you know, though, that *cows* like to dance?'

Jessica shook her head.

'They love the moo-sic!' Olga added.

Jessica burst out laughing.

'I could teach you to juggle,' Jack suggested, pointing at some big pine cones lying on the grass.

Excitedly, Olga picked them up.

'You hold two in one hand and

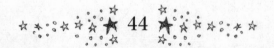

one in the other,' Jack instructed. 'Then you toss one up into the air and as you go to catch it, you throw the next one up.'

Olga threw the first one high into the air. But as it came down again, she missed the catch completely and the enormous pine cone almost hit Wishler on the head.

'I think this is a bit dangerous,' Wishler muttered,

hopping into a hollow in the pine tree to hide.

'Wishler, do you know what trees wear to the swimming pool?' Olga

asked him, getting down on her knees and peering into the hollow.

Wishler shook his head.

'Swimming *trunks*!' Olga chortled loudly.

Wishler laughed so hard that he tumbled out of the tree hollow and into Olga's lap. 'Tell us some more jokes,' he begged, tears rolling down

his pointy face.

'Hey, that's it!' Jack exclaimed. 'I have an idea!'

Chapter
Five

Jack turned to Wishler and Jessica.

'Whenever Olga makes a mistake, she tells a joke,' he pointed out. 'So why doesn't she do a comedy act at the talent competition?'

'That's a brilliant idea, Jack!'

Jessica exclaimed.

But Olga shook her head. 'I don't think I'm very funny,' she said doubtfully.

'Nonsense!' Jessica replied. 'Do you know any more jokes?'

'A few,' Olga said shyly. 'Where do frogs keep their money safe?'

'I don't know,' Jack and Jessica

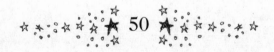

said together.

'A river bank!'

Olga said.

Jack laughed.

He saw a big blue butterfly flutter past them. 'How about a butterfly joke?'

Olga thought briefly. 'Why did the giantess throw the butter-dish

out of the window?' she asked, smiling. 'Because she wanted to see a butter fly!'

Jack, Jessica and Wishler laughed and clapped together.

'Olga, did you just make that up?' Wishler asked admiringly.

Olga nodded, looking very pleased with herself.

Jessica glanced around the forest and saw a giant snail inching its way along. The snail was as big as a Labrador and left a river of sticky slime behind it.

'What about a snail joke?' she asked.

'Sure. Why are snail shells shiny?'

Olga asked. 'Because they use snail varnish!'

'Olga, you've discovered your true talent!' Jessica grinned.

'You could win tonight, Olga,' Wishler added. 'So will you do a comedy act like Jack suggested?'

Olga nodded. 'But I'm a bit scared,' she sighed. 'I can't be funny if I'm

nervous. What if I get stage fright?'

'We'll sit right by your ear and help you,' Jessica reassured her. 'If you freeze, we'll just whisper ideas to get you going again.'

Olga looked a little happier. 'We'd better go straight to the fairground for the talent competition,' she told them. Gently she scooped Jack,

Jessica and Wishler up in one hand
and sat them on her shoulder where
the friends could hide themselves in

her long black hair.

'Off we go!'

Jack, Jessica

and Wishler

all loved

travelling high

on Olga's shoulder. It was like they were sitting on the top of a huge rollercoaster. The giantess's steps were really big and the ground below raced past them.

The fair was taking place in a field just outside the town. There were dodgems, a carousel, a Ferris wheel and other rides. Jack and Jessica

could see that it was just like a fair back home, except that everything was much bigger. The Ferris wheel was as tall as a skyscraper. Jack and Jessica saw a stall with cotton candy as Olga walked by. The soft pink mounds were as big as clouds.

As they passed a popcorn stall, Olga accidentally bumped into

another giant and Jack was sent

flying right off Olga's shoulder.

'Aaahh!' he yelled.

Jessica and Wishler managed to grab on to Olga's hair, and watched in horror as Jack tumbled through the air. 'Olga!' Wishler shouted in the giantess's ear. 'Jack's in trouble!'

Jack gasped as he plummeted right into the middle of a bag of popcorn. The popcorn kernels were as big as tennis balls, which made it a soft landing. 'Phew, that was close!' he thought, peeping out to look for Olga and the others.

'I'll have that one,' a voice said.

The next moment, an enormous hand stretched out towards the bag of popcorn that Jack was hiding in!

Chapter
Six

'Oh no!' Jack groaned, ducking down into the bag and out of sight. Was he about to be eaten by a hungry giant?

Suddenly he heard a voice.

'I think I was next!' Olga huffed. She elbowed aside the customer and

snatched the bag of popcorn Jack was

hiding in.

Jack sighed with relief as Olga

paid the stallholder, then quickly

fished him out of

the bag.

'Thanks, Olga,' Jack whispered, brushing bits of popcorn off his T-shirt.

'You're very welcome,' Olga said. 'I don't suppose you're as tasty as popcorn anyway!'

Jack laughed as Olga placed him carefully on her shoulder again.

'I'm really glad you're all right,

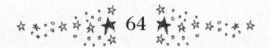

Jack,' Jessica said. 'Who knows what might have happened if that giant had seen you?'

Olga nodded. 'He might have squished you there and then,' she explained, munching her popcorn.

Jack shivered slightly as Olga handed Wishler a giant popcorn kernel for all of them to share.

'I just hope Olga wins the wishing-chair,' he whispered to Jessica, 'and then we can get out of Giantland for good!'

The talent competition was being held on a big stage in the centre of the fairground, and a large audience had already gathered to watch. Olga registered her name backstage, and

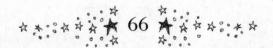

then she went to sit in the audience with Wishler, Jack and Jessica so they could watch the other giants perform.

There was a fanfare of trumpets, and a man in a sparkly suit walked out on to the stage to loud applause. The noise sounded like the loudest thunder imaginable.

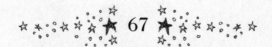

'Look, it's the man who bought the wishing-chair!' Jack murmured.

'Welcome one, welcome all!' the man declared. 'I'm your host, and tonight you're going to see the best talent in all of Giantland.' He grinned. 'And we have a fantastic prize for our winner!' He clicked his fingers and two giants wheeled the

golden throne on to the stage.

The whole audience gasped with

appreciation and clapped again.

'And now, let's meet our first

contestant,' the man went on. 'Put your hands together for Kitty, who sings with the voice of an angel!'

All the giants applauded as Kitty walked on to the stage, but as she began to sing, Jessica winced. Kitty's voice was lovely, but very loud. Olga heaved a deep sigh.

'Kitty has a beautiful voice,' she

whispered to Jack, Jessica and Wishler. 'I'll never beat *her*.'

'You've got just as good a chance of winning,' Jessica told her. But Olga just sighed again.

Kitty was followed by a giant who did a very complicated jig, two more singers, a troupe of acrobats and a giant magician who made a giant

rabbit appear from a top hat. As they watched all these acts, Jack, Jessica and Wishler realised that Olga was becoming more and more gloomy.

'Everyone is so talented,' Olga murmured sadly. 'I'm going to make a fool of myself!'

'No, you're not,' Jack said. 'You're really funny, Olga, I promise.'

The magician took a bow, and the organiser of the competition returned to the stage.

'And now please welcome our comedian, the wonderful Olga!'

The audience applauded as Olga rose from her seat and took to the stage. Jessica could feel the giantess trembling with nerves as she stood

under the spotlights and gazed at all

the people in front of her.

'It's all right, Olga,' said Jessica

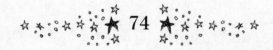

quietly. 'You'll be great!'

'Take a deep breath,' Jack advised the giantess.

Olga did as Jack said. Then she opened her mouth, but no sound came out for a moment or two.

'She's got stage fright!' Jack muttered to Jessica.

'Um – er –' Olga began, fidgeting

uncomfortably. 'I was – er – down in the woods today and – oh, wait a minute, I've forgotten what comes next!'

'You saw a snail,' Wishler prompted.

'Oh, yes,' Olga stumbled on. 'I saw a snail and I said, "How do you get your shell so shiny?" And the snail said, "I use nail varnish."' The giantess shook her head. 'No, that's not right at all!'

From behind the giantess's hair Jack could see the audience begin to shuffle in their seats. A couple of people even started to whisper.

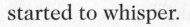

'Come on Olga, you *can* do this,' Jessica said.

'Er – forget the snail!' Olga said, suddenly standing a bit straighter. 'I went into the woods and I met a frog carrying a bag full of money. I said, "Mr Frog, how do you keep your money safe?" And he croaked, "I put it in the river bank!"'

This time there was a ripple of laughter from the audience.

'Anyway, while I was in the woods, I asked the pine trees if they'd like to come to my pool party,' Olga went on. 'I told them to bring along their swimming trunks!'

There was more laughter, and Jack, Jessica and Wishler beamed happily

at each other.

Olga seemed to forget about her stage fright and went flying through her routine, keeping the audience in fits of laughter. She finished off with the butterfly joke and took a bow, but the audience began calling out, 'More! More!' and chanting her name over and over again.

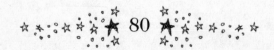

'What shall I do?' Olga whispered anxiously to Jack, Jessica and Wishler.

'Make up some more jokes,' Jack said, remembering how Olga had done the same thing in the forest. 'Try a joke about . . .' He glanced at the audience and saw a man eating a banana. 'A banana!'

Olga turned back to the audience.

'Well, I went to the doctor the other day and I met a banana there. He said he wasn't peeling very well!'

The audience roared with laughter again. Jack, Jessica and Wishler grinned happily.

'Keep making suggestions,' Jack whispered to his sister and Wishler.

'Hippopotamus!' Jessica said in Olga's ear.

'Let me tell you about the time I walked with a hippopotamus,' Olga

began. Then she went on to make up lots of new jokes as Jack, Jessica and Wishler whispered words like *measles, library* and *buttons* in her ear. Soon Olga was telling jokes so quickly, about all sorts of subjects, that she didn't need Jack, Jessica and Wishler's help at all.

The audience were laughing and

holding their sides. They gave Olga a

standing ovation as she took a bow

and left the stage.

'And now for the results!' said the host, as he came on stage wiping tears of laughter from his eyes. 'I think we agree that everyone performed superbly tonight. But there can only be one winner . . .'

'Let's hope it's Olga,' Jessica whispered, crossing her fingers.

'The winner of tonight's Grand

Prize is . . . Olga, our comedian!' the host declared.

The audience erupted into cheers. Olga's mouth fell open in surprise.

'You did it, Olga!' Jack cheered.

'Well done!' Wishler exclaimed.

'I couldn't have done it without you,' Olga whispered back, beaming. 'Thank you.' She went on stage to

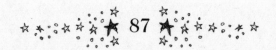

be presented with a glittering golden crown, as well as the golden throne.

'And we have another extra-special prize for our winner,' the host announced. 'Olga, you will now go straight to the Royal Tent to perform for the King and Queen of Giantland!'

'Oh!' Olga clasped her hands and

squealed in excitement.

Jack smiled at Wishler and Jessica.

'Olga really *has* found her talent!'

he said happily.

Jack, Jessica and Wishler watched as the golden throne was carried backstage, Olga following behind it.

'Thank you again,' Olga said gratefully, when they were alone. She bent down so that Jack, Jessica and Wishler could hop off her shoulder. Then Wishler tapped the throne and said, 'Show yourself!'

Suddenly the throne disappeared and there was the wishing-chair, looking very tiny next to Olga.

'I'm looking forward to going home,' Jack said quietly to Jessica as they sat down. 'I've had enough of being tiny!'

'Me too,' Jessica agreed. 'We're lucky we haven't been squished like

bugs with all the giants around!'

But suddenly Olga reached down and swept the three friends up in her hand. Then she grabbed the tiny wishing-chair in the other.

'Olga!' Wishler gasped. 'What are you doing?'

'You *can't* go home,' Olga said firmly. 'Not ever!'

Chapter Seven

'What?' Jessica said, horrified.

Olga looked very uncomfortable. 'I can't perform for the King and Queen without you to help me,' she explained. 'And what if people ask me to do more performances?'

'Olga, we want to go home now –' Jack began.

But Olga ignored him. She slipped the wishing-chair into her pocket. Then she opened a pretty lattice locket that hung round her neck.

'You'll be able to see out through the lattice,' she told Jack, Jessica and Wishler as she put them inside

the locket. Then, before they could

escape, she clicked it shut.

'Olga!' Jack yelled, banging on the

side of the locket. 'Let us out!'

'Olga's just scared,' Jessica said

understandingly.

'She doesn't

think she

can be funny

without us to help her.'

'She's going to keep us here forever so that we can give her ideas for jokes!' Jack shouted crossly as the host of the contest led Olga towards the Royal Tent.

Wishler shook his head. 'We helped Olga find her talent, but not her confidence.'

Jack sighed. 'OK then we have to make Olga see that she can be funny all on her own,' he said. 'Or we might *never* get home!'

'How?' Jessica asked.

'Well, if we don't help her, Olga will have to perform on her own, won't she?' Jack said. 'So all we do is keep quiet. Don't say a word!'

Jessica and Wishler nodded in agreement.

When they reached the purple and gold Royal Tent, the three friends peered out of the locket. The host had taken Olga backstage, but through a tiny hole in the curtains Jack, Jessica and Wishler could see the giant King and Queen sitting on their huge

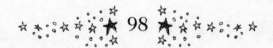

thrones. Along either side of the tent sat the courtiers and royal guests. Suddenly, there was a burst of music and a page stepped forward.

'Your Majesties,' he announced. 'We present the winner of the talent competition – Olga the comedian!'

Quickly Olga opened the locket and sat Jack, Jessica and Wishler on

her shoulder. Then she stepped confidently out on to the stage.

'Your Majesties, I'm honoured to be performing for you tonight,' Olga began, curtseying very low. She stopped, waiting for suggestions. But Jack, Jessica and Wishler kept silent.

'Er – I have lots of new jokes to tell you,' Olga said. But still Jack, Jessica

and Wishler said nothing.

'Help me!' Olga whispered out of the side of her mouth. She cleared her throat. 'Um – do forgive me,

Your Majesties, but I – er – forgot something!' And then she dashed out of the tent. Jessica could hear the crowd grumbling as Olga left.

Backstage Olga scooped Jack, Jessica and Wishler off her shoulder and stared down at them as they stood in her hand. 'Please help me!' she begged.

Jack shook his head. 'You promised we could go home, but you've gone back on your word.'

'I'll give you the wishing-chair right after the show, if you'll help me first,' Olga pleaded.

But Jack shook his head again. 'You broke your promise once,' he said. 'I'm just not sure we can trust you any more.'

Olga immediately burst into loud sobs, large tears welling in her eyes.

'Don't cry, Olga!' Wishler called in alarm, jumping aside as a huge splash  of water plopped down right next to him. 'You don't really need us to help you.' 'What do you mean?'

Olga gulped through her tears.

'*You're* the one who makes up all the jokes,' Wishler explained. '*You're* the funny one!'

'If you can't think of anything,' Jack continued, 'why not ask the King and Queen and the rest of the audience to suggest things you can make jokes about?'

Olga smiled. 'What a wonderful idea!'

Suddenly, Wishler flickered in and out of focus.

'Oh no,' Jessica said. 'We really have to go. The wishing-chair is getting impatient and might leave without us!'

Chapter Eight

'The wishing-chair isn't going anywhere without you,' Olga declared, putting the three friends down on a nearby table. 'I'm sorry I broke my promise before.'

She placed the wishing-chair next

to them. 'You've been really great friends, and I hope you'll come back and visit me again.'

'We will,' Jessica said with a grin. 'Now go on, the King and Queen are waiting!'

Jack, Jessica and Wishler waved goodbye as Olga ran back into the Royal Tent.

'Your Majesties,' they heard Olga announce. 'Give me a subject – any subject – and I'll tell you a joke.'

'Beanstalk,' the King called.

'Why is there always so much noise in the garden?' Olga enquired. 'Because Jack and the beans talk!'

Jack, Jessica and Wishler laughed along with everyone in the audience.

'Olga's going to do just fine!' said Wishler. 'It's time to go.'

They began to rock the chair to and

fro as blue sparks appeared.

'Home!' Jack called, closing his

eyes as the sparks shot from the

chair's rockers. They whizzed into the air, falling almost immediately back to earth again.

'We're home!' Jessica exclaimed, opening her eyes and staring around the garden shed. 'Isn't it *great* to be surrounded by normal-sized things?'

Jack and Wishler nodded.

'It was kind of fun being a little

person for a while,' Jack said with a grin, 'but it was scary too!'

Jessica jumped off the wishing-chair. 'I'd better go and practise for my audition,' she said. 'At least I know exactly how the people of Lilliput felt when they met Gulliver!'

Jack opened his mouth, then shook his head and shut it again.

'What were you going to say, Jack?' Wishler asked curiously.

'I was going to make a joke about Jessica's audition,' Jack said with a shrug. 'But I think we've all had enough jokes for one day!'

EGMONT PRESS: ETHICAL PUBLISHING

Egmont Press is about turning writers into successful authors and children into passionate readers – producing books that enrich and entertain. As a responsible children's publisher, we go even further, considering the world in which our consumers are growing up.

Safety First
Naturally, all of our books meet legal safety requirements. But we go further than this; every book with play value is tested to the highest standards – if it fails, it's back to the drawing-board.

Made Fairly
We are working to ensure that the workers involved in our supply chain – the people that make our books – are treated with fairness and respect.

Responsible Forestry
We are committed to ensuring all our papers come from environmentally and socially responsible forest sources.

**For more information, please visit our website at
www.egmont.co.uk/ethical**